As Josie sleeps, the Dark Man stands at the edge of the river.

It is dark, and the rain is lashing down.

On the far side, the nice part of the city is brightly lit.

The Dark Man looks down and sees the rain splashing hard on the water.

The Dark Man has been to this place before.

Last time, Josie was with him.

Back then, she showed him where to find the Dark Bridge.

A breeze blows across the water.

For a moment, the Dark Man seems to see Josie's face reflected on the surface.

The Dark Bridge is gone, but the river can still do harm.

There is something beneath the waters of the river that he must find.

Seven gold coins, made from the same piece of gold as the magical Golden Cup.

This gold is special.

Pieces of it will always try to come together, to make one solid ingot again.

The Old Man said that the coins can help them find the Golden Cup.

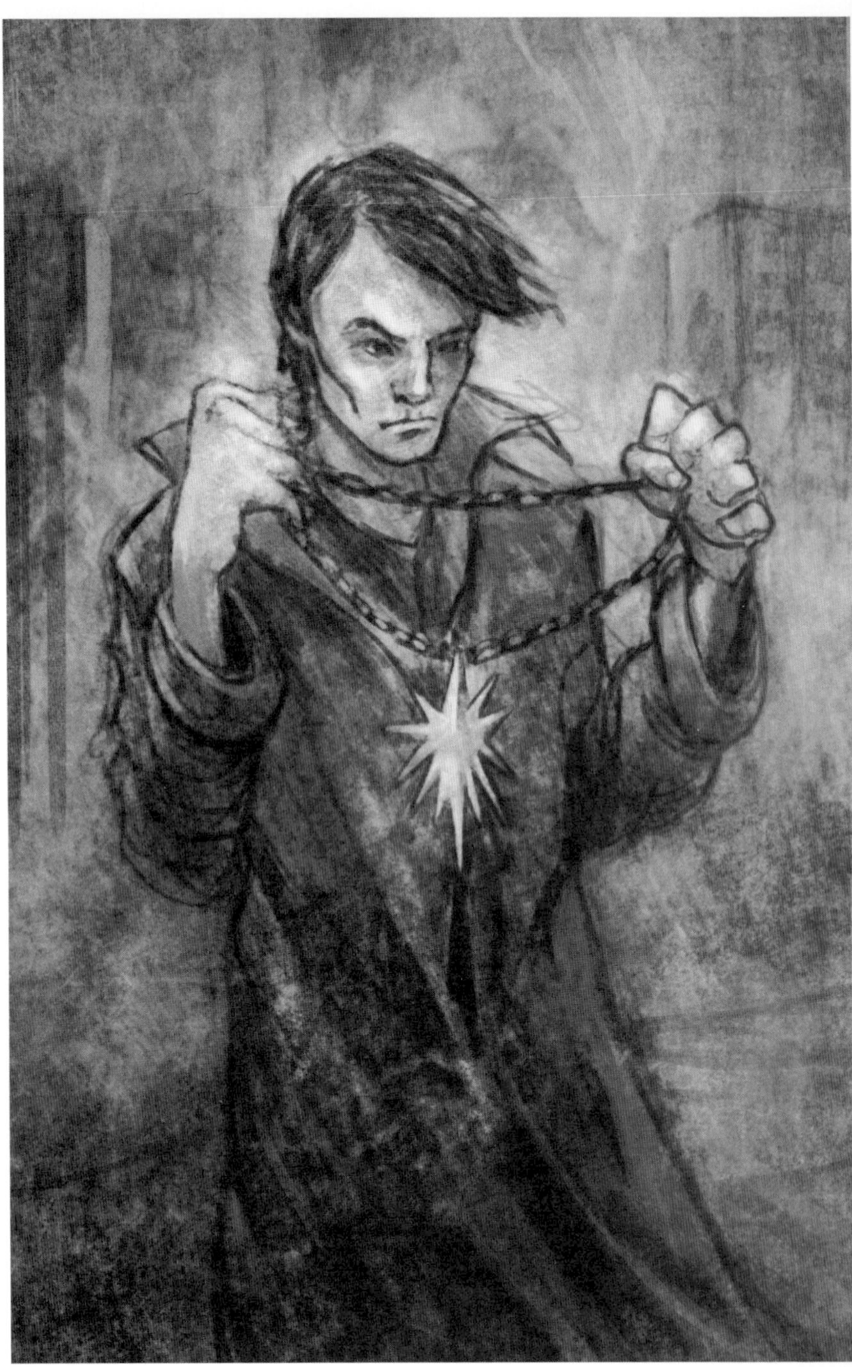

The Dark Man takes a silver star and chain from his pocket.

He puts it around his neck.

The Old Man said that the silver star will give him power to see in the dark.

It will be pitch black beneath the water.

Chapter Two:
The Gold Coins

Long ago, the Old Man showed the Dark Man a special way of breathing.

It is an ancient method, long forgotten.

It will allow him to stay beneath the water for a long time.

The Dark Man begins to breathe, in the way that the Old Man showed him.

He breathes long and deep.

At last, he is ready.

The rain has already soaked him, so he keeps his clothes on and slips into the dark water below.

His coat swirls around him as his feet find the riverbed.

The water is cold. He cannot see anything.

The silver star does not seem to be working.

He turns his head, this way and that.

Something unseen brushes against his face.

He turns to look, but the water is too dark.

Then he sees something shimmering in the distance, holding still against the flow of the water.

He strides toward this faint light.

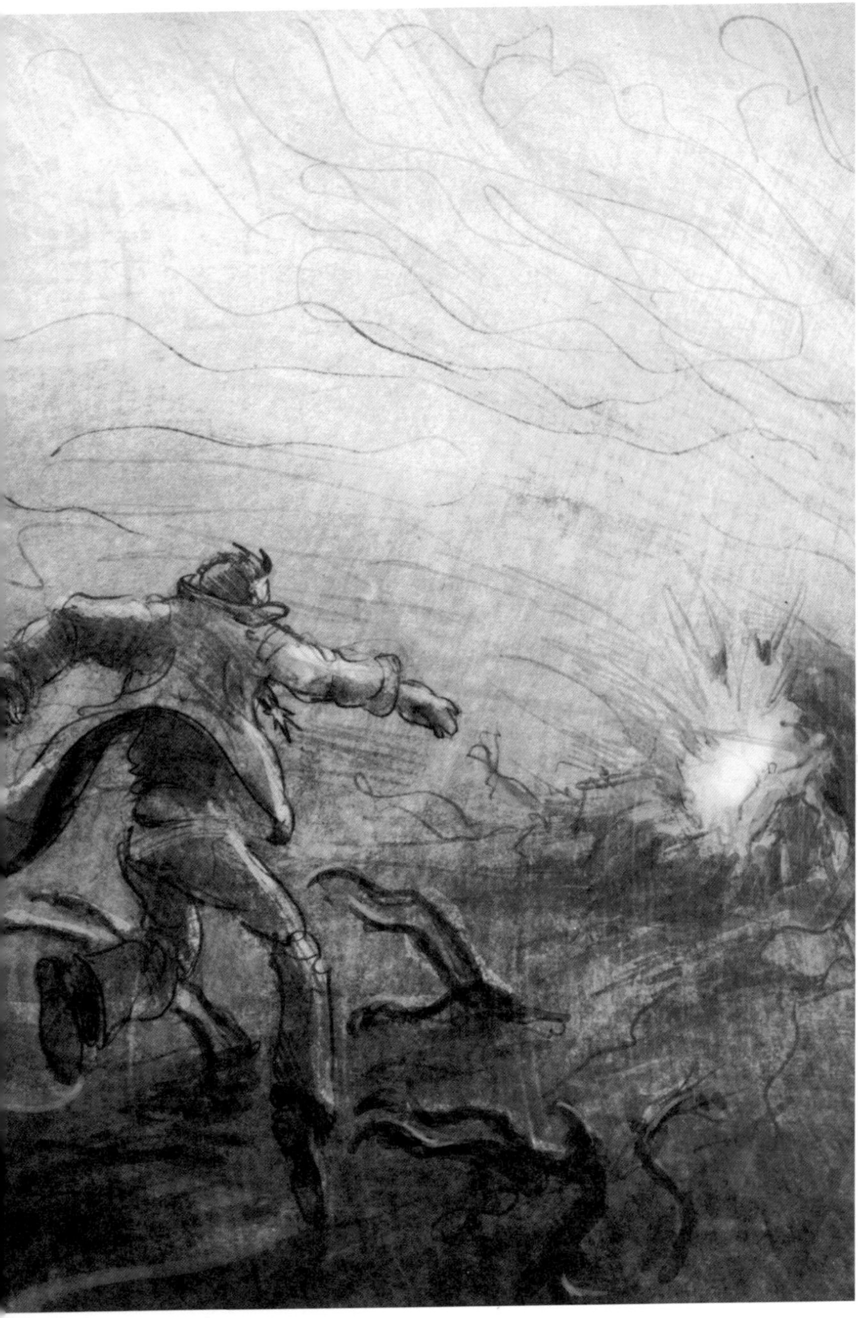

As he approaches the light, the silver star around his neck begins to feel warm against his skin.

Then, closer, he can see what the light is.

It is Josie's face, floating like a ghost in the water.

And the face is smiling.

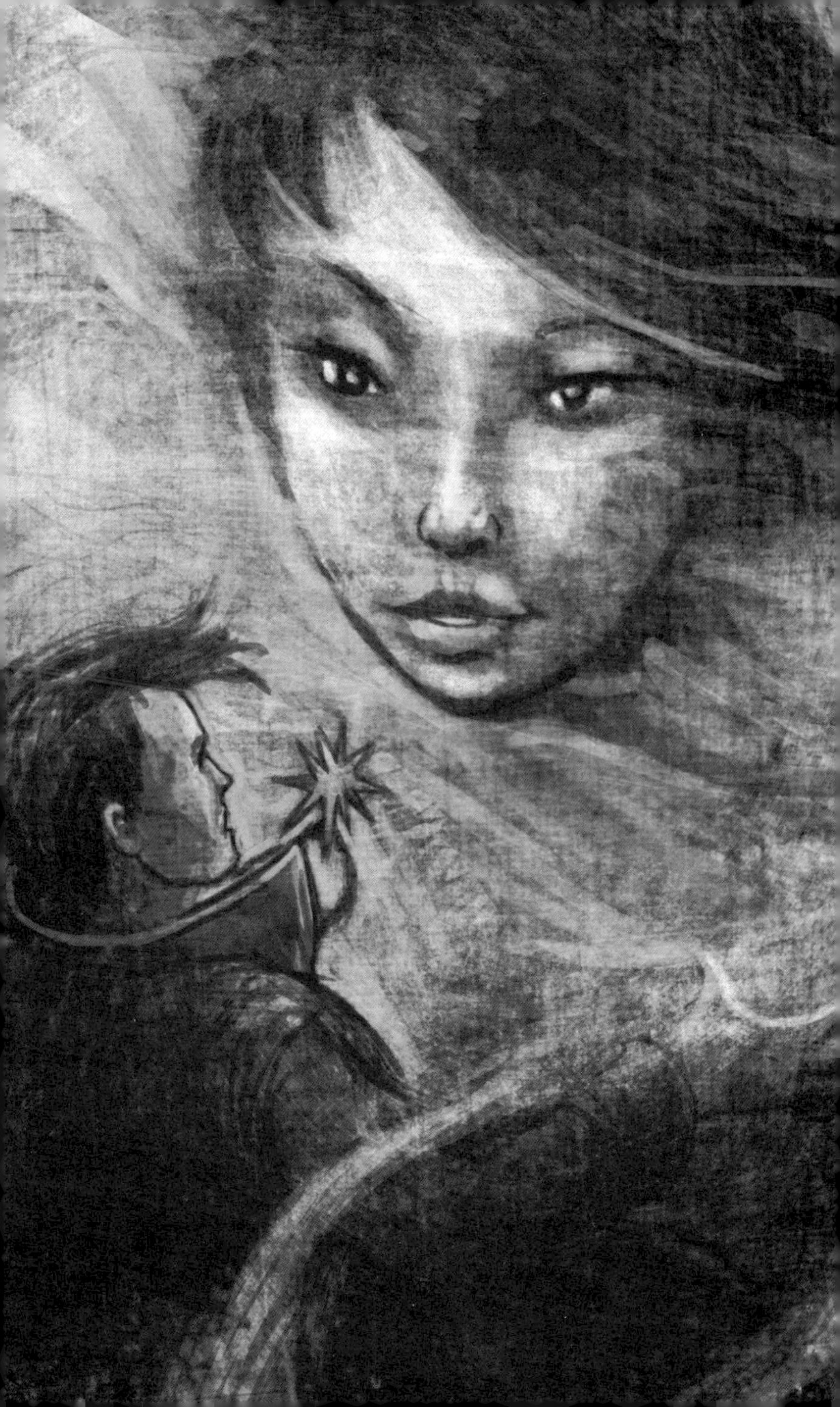

He strides toward the face, and suddenly the water becomes clear.

He can see everything.

The face looks down, to the riverbed below.

The Dark Man follows this gaze.

There are massive rocks on the riverbed.

One is black and has a huge hole in it.

Yellow light seems to be coming from this hole.

It must be the gold coins!

Josie is showing him where they are.

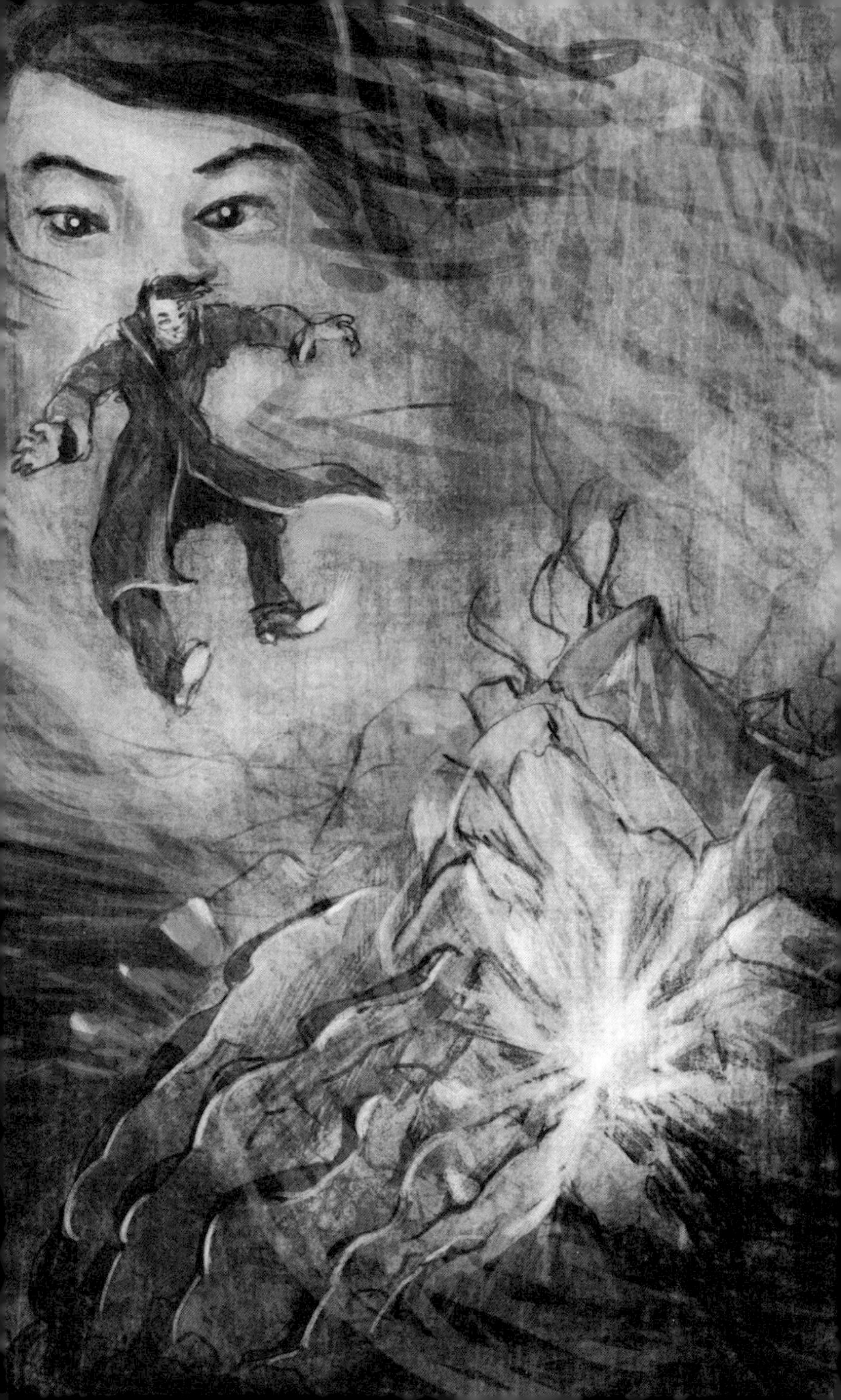

Chapter Three:
Three Girls

All of a sudden, light begins to shimmer from behind the rock.

As the Dark Man watches, three girls rise slowly in the water.

The girls are lovely.

They wear clothes and makeup under the water.

They look just like girls from the city.

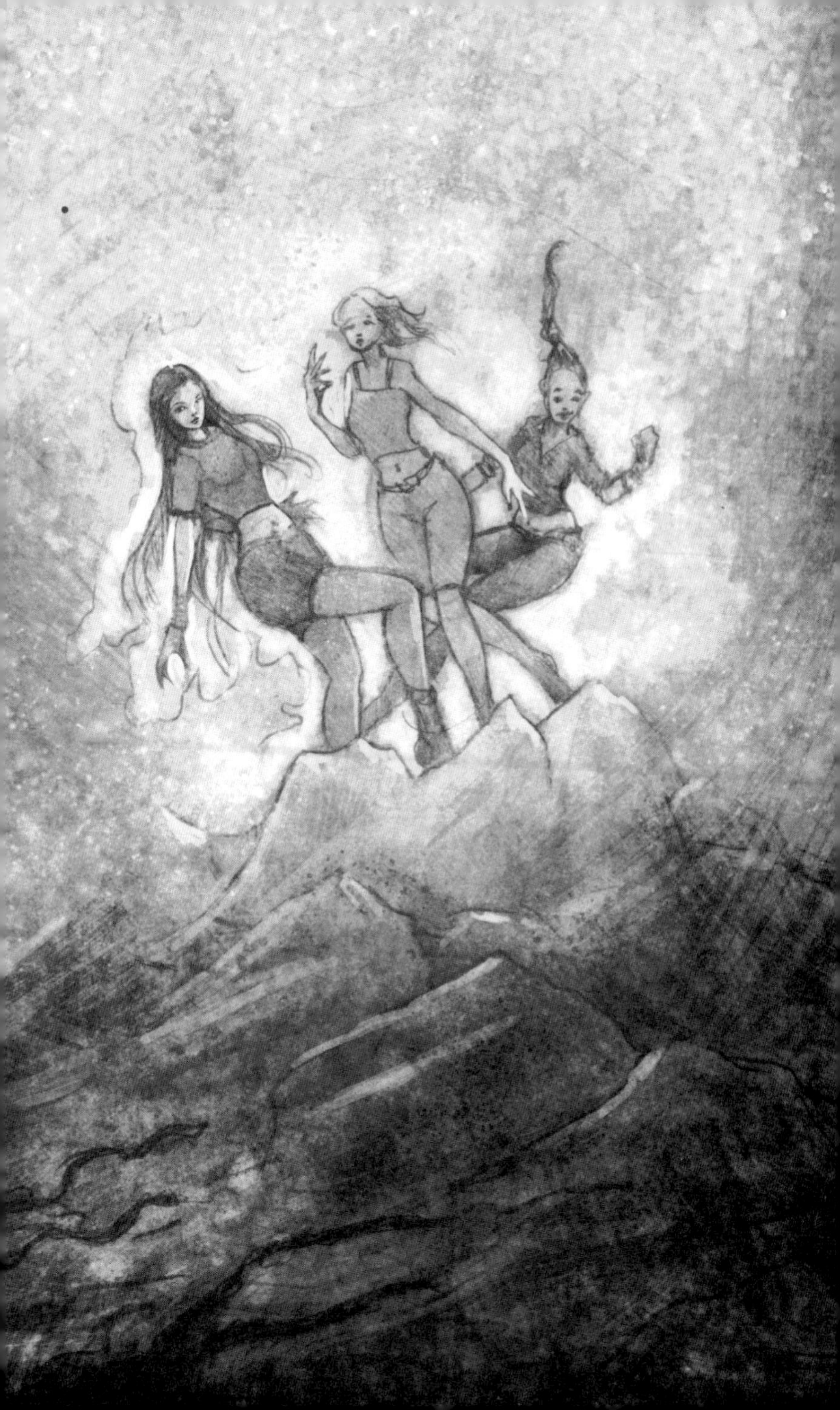

The Dark Man watches as these girls glide through the water.

They seem to be playing, darting here and there.

Sometimes they come close and brush against him.

As the Dark Man glances around, he notices that the ghostly face of Josie no longer smiles.

This reminds him that he has come here for the gold coins.

He cannot stay below the water forever.

He stoops to reach inside the rock.

The coins are lying together.

Each one is in a small canvas bag.

The Dark Man tries to pick one bag up.

He cannot move it.

He has to give up trying.

A savage roar rips through the water.

The Dark Man turns.

The ghostly face of Josie is no longer smiling.

Around her, the playful girls are changing.

As the Dark Man watches, the girls melt into the water of the river.

Then suddenly, they become terrible creatures, with sharp teeth and talons.

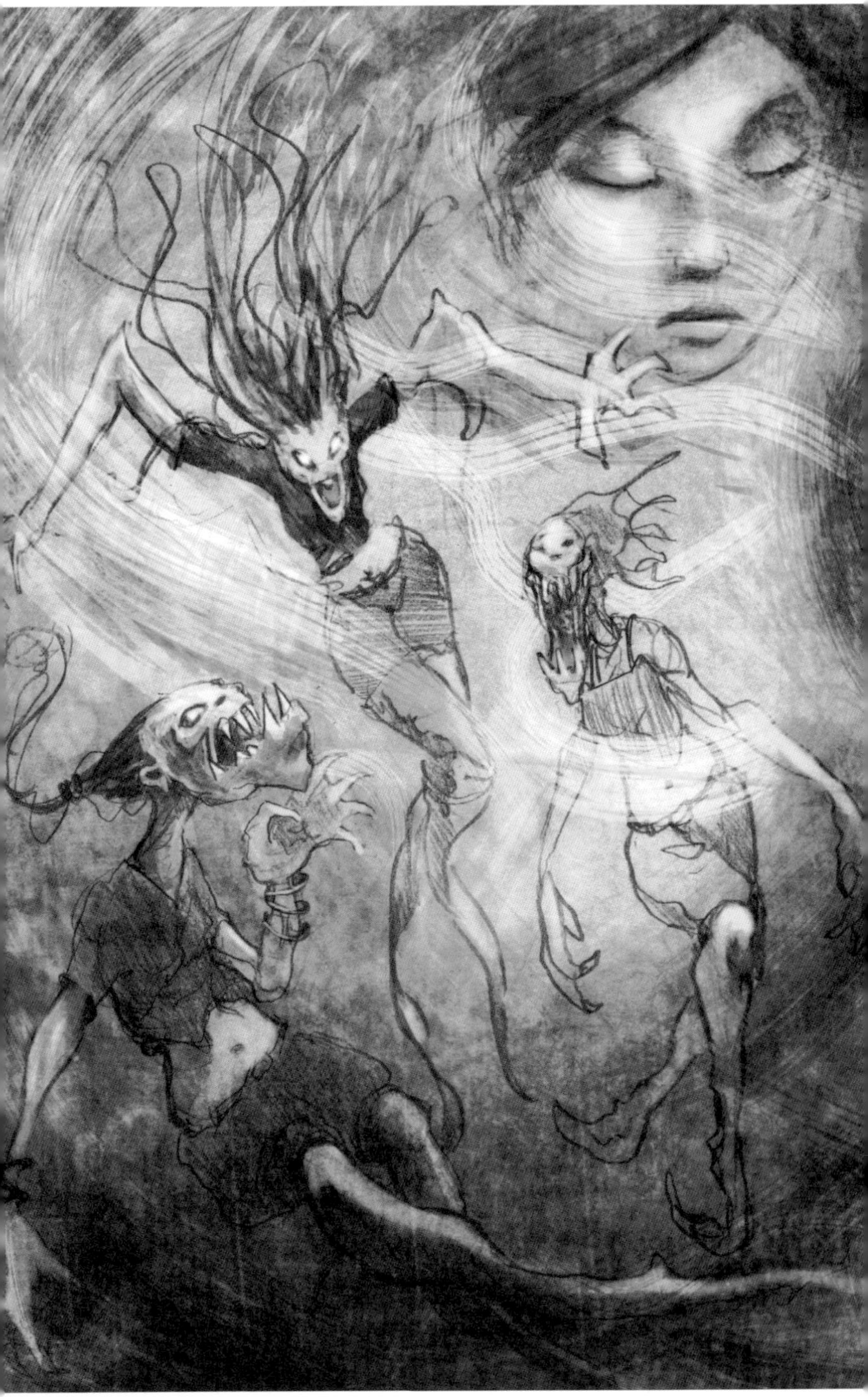

The Dark Man is going to need air soon.

Once again, he reaches for the coins.

He cannot move any of them.

The savage creatures snap and slash at him as they swim by.

He is strong enough to brush them away.

But his lungs are bursting, and he needs to breathe.

He cannot leave the gold coins.

Then he remembers.

The gold in these coins is magical.

All parts of it want to come together.

He will have to gather them all up at the same time.

Now though, he cannot reach for them.

He has to fight off the savage river creatures.

His lungs are on fire.

He will have to breathe soon.

Just before he has to fight his way to the surface, a rainbow of light starts to glow around him.

The ghostly figure of Josie stands next to him.

Josie is smiling, and the creatures seem afraid of her smile.

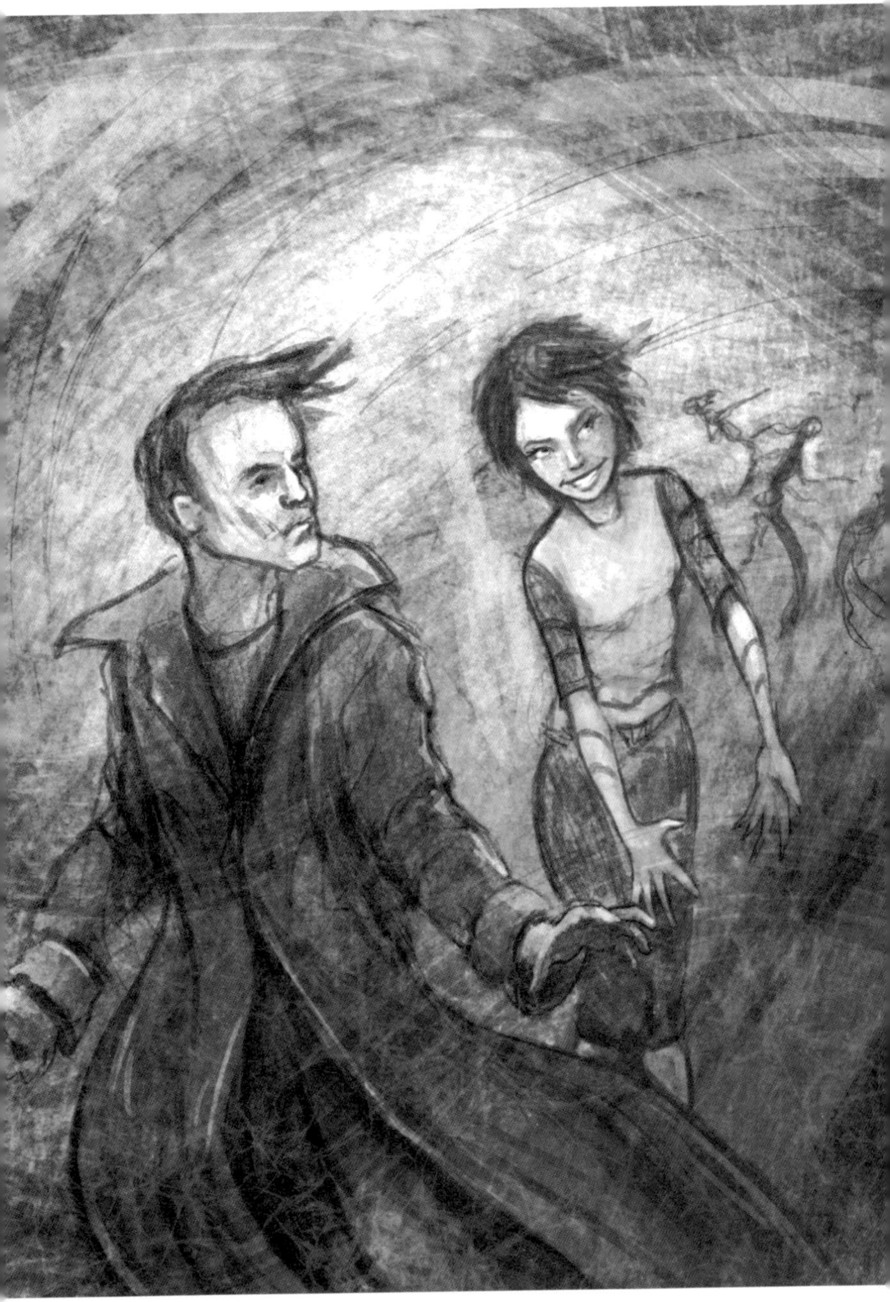

The Dark Man reaches into the rock one last time and gathers all the coins at the same time.

With the coin bags held in one hand, he swims for the surface.

He bursts into the air, gasping for breath.

In his hand, he still holds the gold coins.

Chapter Four:
Josie

In the bedroom where Josie lies sleeping,
the Dark Man stands at the foot of the bed.

His clothes are still dripping with water
from the river.

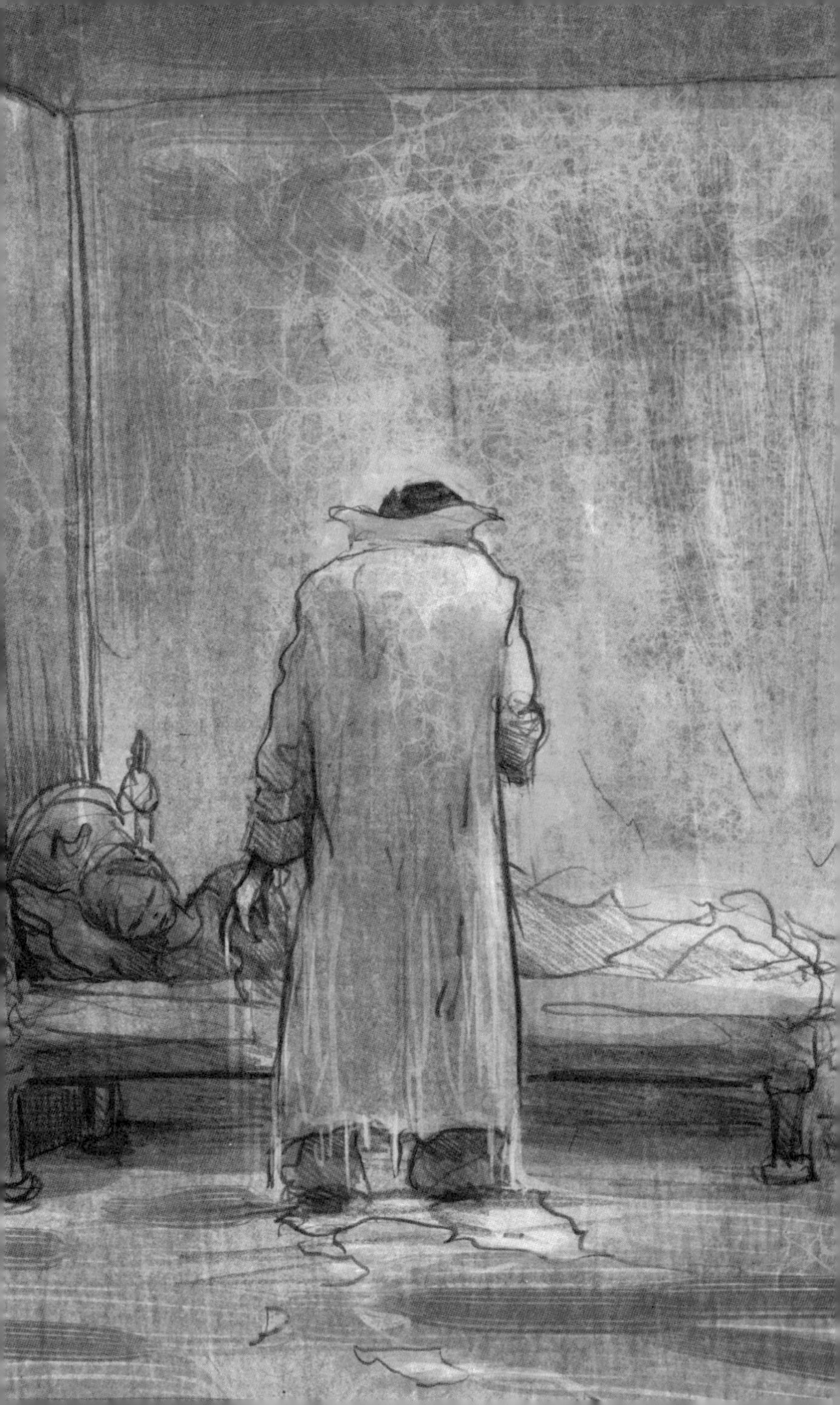

Josie stirs, and her sad face sees him there.

"I was dreaming of you," she says.

"I know," he replies. "I have just come to see that you are safe."

He watches as she drifts back into sleep,
then quietly leaves.

He walks down the street, alone.

Tomorrow, he will deliver the coins to the Old Man.

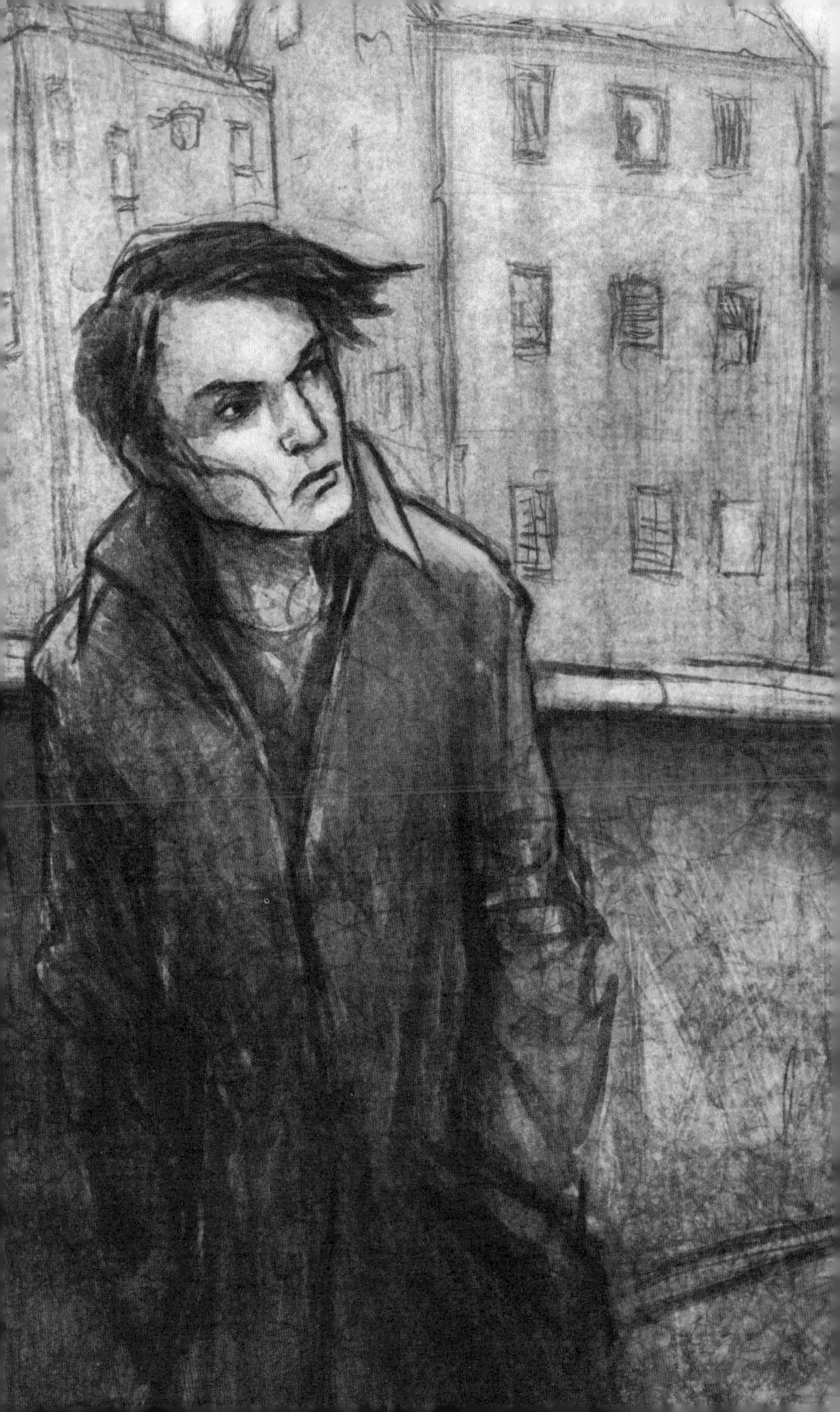

THE AUTHOR

Peter Lancett is a writer, editor, and filmmaker. He has written many books and has just made a feature film, *The Xlitherman*.

Peter now lives in New Zealand and California.